Pauline's Passion and Punishment

Louisa May Alcott

Contents

Chapter I..7

Chapter II 14

Chapter III...28

Chapter IV 39

PAULINE'S PASSION AND PUNISHMENT

BY

Louisa May Alcott

Chapter I

To and fro, like a wild creature in its cage, paced that handsome woman, with bent head, locked hands, and restless steps. Some mental storm, swift and sudden as a tempest of the tropics, had swept over her and left its marks behind. As if in anger at the beauty now proved powerless, all ornaments had been flung away, yet still it shone undimmed, and filled her with a passionate regret. A jewel glittered at her feet, leaving the lace rent to shreds on the indignant bosom that had worn it; the wreaths of hair that had crowned her with a woman's most womanly adornment fell disordered upon shoulders that gleamed the fairer for the scarlet of the pomegranate flowers clinging to the bright meshes that had imprisoned them an hour ago; and over the face, once so affluent in youthful bloom, a stern pallor had fallen like a blight, for pride was slowly conquering passion, and despair had murdered hope.

Pausing in her troubled march, she swept away the curtain swaying in the wind and looked out, as if imploring help from Nature, the great mother of us all. A summer moon rode high in a cloudless heaven, and far as eye could reach stretched the green wilderness of a Cuban *cafetal*. No forest, but a tropical orchard, rich in lime, banana, plantain, palm, and orange trees, under whose protective shade grew the evergreen coffee plant, whose dark-red berries are the fortune of their possessor, and the luxury of one-half the world. Wide avenues diverging from the mansion, with its belt of brilliant shrubs and flowers, formed shadowy vistas, along which, on the wings of the wind, came a breath of far-off music, like a wooing voice; for the magic of night and distance lulled the cadence of a Spanish *contradanza* to a trance of sound, soft, subdued, and infinitely sweet. It was a southern scene, but not a southern face that looked out upon it with such unerring glance; there was no southern languor in the figure, stately and erect; no southern swarthiness on fairest cheek and arm; no southern darkness in the shadowy gold of the neglected hair; the light frost of northern snows lurked in the features, delicately cut, yet vividly alive, betraying a temperament ardent, dominant, and subtle. For passion burned in the deep eyes, changing their violet to black. Pride sat on the forehead, with its dark brows; all a woman's sweetest spells touched the lips, whose shape was a smile; and in the spirited carriage of the head appeared the freedom of an intellect ripened under colder skies, the energy of a nature that could wring strength from suffering, and dare to act where feebler souls would only dare desire.

Standing thus, conscious only of the wound that bled in that high heart of hers, and the longing that gradually took shape and deepened to a purpose, an alien presence changed the tragic atmosphere of that still room and woke her from her dangerous mood. A wonderfully winning guise this apparition wore, for youth, hope, and love endowed it with the charm that gives beauty to the plainest, while their reign endures. A boy in any other climate, in this his nineteen years had given him the stature of a man; and Spain, the land of romance, seemed embodied in this figure, full of the lithe slenderness of the whispering palms overhead, the warm coloring of the deep-toned flowers sleeping in the room, the native grace of the tame antelope lifting its human eyes to his as he lingered on the threshold in an attitude eager yet timid, watching that other figure as it looked into the night and found no solace there.

"Pauline!"

She turned as if her thought had taken voice and answered her, regarded him a moment, as if hesitating to receive the granted wish, then beckoned with the one word.

"Come!"

Instantly the fear vanished, the ardor deepened, and with an imperious "Lie down!" to his docile attendant, the young man obeyed with equal docility, looking as wistfully toward his mistress as the brute toward her master, while he waited proudly humble for her commands.

"Manuel, why are you here?"

"Forgive me! I saw Dolores bring a letter; you vanished, an hour passed, I could wait no longer, and I came."

"I am glad, I needed my one friend. Read that."

She offered a letter, and with her steady eyes upon him, her purpose strengthening as she looked, stood watching the changes of that expressive countenance. This was the letter:

Pauline--

Six months ago I left you, promising to return and take you home my wife; I loved you, but I deceived you; for though my heart was wholly yours, my hand was not mine to give. This it was that haunted me through all that blissful summer, this that marred my happiness when you owned you loved me, and this drove me from you, hoping I could break the tie with which I had rashly bound myself. I could not, I am married, and there all ends. Hate me, forget me, solace your pride with the memory that none knew your wrong, assure your peace with the knowledge that mine is destroyed forever, and leave my punishment to remorse and time.

Gilbert

With a gesture of wrathful contempt, Manuel flung the paper from him as he flashed a look at his companion, muttering through his teeth, "Traitor! Shall I kill him?"

Pauline laughed low to herself, a dreary sound, but answered with a slow darkening of the face that gave her words an ominous significance. "Why should you? Such revenge is brief and paltry, fit only for mock tragedies or poor souls who have neither the will to devise nor the will to execute a better. There are fates more terrible than death; weapons more keen than poniards, more noiseless than pistols. Women use such, and work out a subtler vengeance than men can conceive. Leave Gilbert to remorse--and me."

She paused an instant, and by some strong effort banished the black frown from her brow, quenched the baleful fire of her eyes, and left nothing visible but the pale determination that made her beautiful face more eloquent than her words.

"Manuel, in a week I leave the island."

"Alone, Pauline?"

"No, not alone."

A moment they looked into each other's eyes, each endeavoring to read the other. Manuel saw some indomitable purpose, bent on conquering all obstacles. Pauline saw doubt, desire, and hope; knew that a word would bring the ally she needed; and, with a courage as native to her as her pride, resolved to utter it.

Seating herself, she beckoned her companion to assume the place beside her, but for the first time he hesitated. Something in the unnatural calmness of her manner troubled him, for his southern temperament was alive to influences whose presence would have been unfelt by one less sensitive. He took the cushion at her feet, saying, half tenderly, half reproachfully, "Let me keep my old place till I know in what character I am to fill the new. The man you trusted has deserted you; the boy you pitied will prove loyal. Try him, Pauline."

"I will."

And with the bitter smile unchanged upon her lips, the low voice unshaken in its tones, the deep eyes unwavering in their gaze, Pauline went on:

"You know my past, happy as a dream till eighteen. Then all was swept away, home, fortune, friends, and I was left, like an unfledged bird, without even the shelter of a cage. For five years I have made my life what I could, humble, honest, but never happy, till I came here, for here I saw Gilbert. In the poor companion of your guardian's daughter he seemed to see the heiress I had been, and treated me as such. This flattered my pride and touched my heart. He was kind, I grateful; then he loved me, and God knows how utterly I loved him! A few months of happiness the purest, then he went to make home ready for me, and I believed him; for where I wholly love I wholly trust. While my own peace was undisturbed, I learned to read the language of your eyes, Manuel, to find the boy grown into the man, the friend warmed into a lover. Your youth had kept me blind too long. Your society had grown dear to me, and I loved you like a sister for your unvarying kindness to the solitary woman who earned her bread and found it bitter. I told you my secret to prevent the utterance of your own. You remember the promise you made me then, keep it still, and bury the knowledge of my lost happiness deep in your pitying heart, as I shall in my proud one. Now the storm is over, and I am ready for my work again, but it must be a new task in a new scene. I hate this house, this room, the faces I must meet, the duties I must perform, for the memory of that traitor haunts them all. I see a future full of interest, a stage whereon I could play a stirring part. I long for it intensely, yet cannot make it mine alone. Manuel, do you love me still?"

Bending suddenly, she brushed back the dark hair that streaked his forehead and searched the face that in an instant answered her. Like a swift rising light, the eloquent blood rushed over swarthy cheek and brow, the slumberous softness of the eyes kindled with a flash, and the lips, sensitive as any woman's, trembled yet broke into a rapturous smile as he cried, with fervent brevity, "I would die for you!"

A look of triumph swept across her face, for with this boy, as chivalrous as ardent, she knew that words were not mere breath. Still, with her stern purpose uppermost, she changed the bitter smile into one half-timid, half-tender, as she bent still nearer, "Manuel, in a week I leave the island. Shall I go alone?"

"No, Pauline."

He understood her now. She saw it in the sudden paleness that fell on him, heard it in the rapid beating of his heart, felt it in the strong grasp that fastened on her hand, and knew that the first step was won. A regretful pang smote her, but the dark mood which had taken possession of her stifled the generous warnings of her better self and drove her on.

"Listen, Manuel. A strange spirit rules me tonight, but I will have no reserves from you, all shall be told; then, if you will come, be it so; if not, I shall go my way as solitary as I came. If you think that this loss has broken my heart, undeceive yourself, for such as I live years in an hour and show no sign. I have shed no tears, uttered no cry, asked no comfort; yet, since I read that letter, I have suffered more than many suffer in a lifetime. I am not one to lament long over any hopeless sorrow. A single paroxysm, sharp and short, and it is over. Contempt has killed my love, I have buried it, and no power can make it live again, except as a pale ghost that will not rest till Gilbert shall pass through an hour as bitter as the last."

"Is that the task you give yourself, Pauline?"

The savage element that lurks in southern blood leaped up in the boy's heart as he listened, glittered in his eye, and involuntarily found expression in the nervous grip of the hands that folded a fairer one between them. Alas for Pauline that she had roused the sleeping devil, and was glad to see it!

"Yes, it is weak, wicked, and unwomanly; yet I persist as relentlessly as any Indian on a war trail. See me as I am, not the gay girl you have known, but a revengeful woman with but one tender spot now left in her heart, the place you fill. I have been wronged, and I long to right myself at once. Time is too slow; I cannot wait, for that man must be taught that two can play at the game of hearts, taught soon and sharply. I can do this, can wound as I have been wounded, can sting him with contempt, and prove that I too can forget."

"Go on, Pauline. Show me how I am to help you."

"Manuel, I want fortune, rank, splendor, and power; you can give me all these, and a faithful friend beside. I desire to show Gilbert the creature he deserted no longer poor, unknown, unloved, but lifted higher than himself, cherished, honored, applauded, her life one of royal pleasure, herself a happy queen. Beauty, grace, and talent you tell me I possess; wealth gives them luster, rank exalts them, power makes them irresistible. Place these worldly gifts in my hand and that hand is yours. See, I offer it."

She did so, but it was not taken. Manuel had left his seat and now stood before her, awed by the undertone of strong emotion in her calmly spoken words, bewildered by the proposal so abruptly made, longing to ask the natural question hovering on his lips, yet too generous to utter it. Pauline read his thought, and answered it with no touch of pain or pride in the magical voice that seldom spoke in vain.

"I know your wish; it is as just as your silence is generous, and I reply to it in all sincerity. You would ask, 'When I have given all that I possess, what do I receive in return?' This--a wife whose friendship is as warm as many a woman's love; a wife who will give you all the heart still left her, and cherish the hope that time may bring a harvest of real affection to repay you for the faithfulness of years; who, though she takes the retribution of a wrong into her hands and executes it in the face of heaven, never will forget the honorable name you give into her keeping or blemish it by any act of hers. I can promise no more. Will this content you, Manuel?"

Before she ended his face was hidden in his hands, and tears streamed through them as he listened, for like a true child of the south each emotion found free vent and spent itself as swiftly as it rose. The reaction was more than he could bear, for in a moment his life was changed, months of hopeless longing were banished with a word, a blissful yes canceled the hard no that had been accepted as inexorable, and Happiness, lifting her full cup to his lips, bade him drink. A moment he yielded to the natural relief, then dashed his tears away and threw himself at Pauline's feet in that attitude fit only for a race as graceful as impassioned.

"Forgive me! Take all I have--fortune, name, and my poor self; use us as you will, we are proud and happy to be spent for you! No service will be too hard, no trial too long if in the end you learn to love me with one tithe of the affection I have made my life. Do you mean it? Am I to go with you? To be near you always, to call you wife, and know we are each other's until death? What have I ever done to earn a fate like this?"

Fast and fervently he spoke, and very winsome was the glad abandonment of this young lover, half boy, half man, possessing the simplicity of the one, the fervor of the other. Pauline looked and listened with a soothing sense of consolation in the knowledge that this loyal heart was all her own, a sweet foretaste of the devotion which henceforth was to shelter her from poverty, neglect, and wrong, and turn life's sunniest side to one who had so long seen only its most bleak and barren. Still at her feet, his arms about her waist, his face flushed and proud, lifted to hers, Manuel saw the cold mask soften, the stern eyes melt with a sudden dew as Pauline watched him, saying, "Dear Manuel, love me less; I am not worth such ardent and entire faith. Pause and reflect before you take this step. I will not bind you to my fate too soon lest you repent too late. We both stand alone in the world, free to make or mar our future as we will. I have chosen my lot. Recall all it may cost you to share it and be sure the price is not too high a one. Remember I am poor, you the possessor of one princely fortune, the sole heir to another."

"The knowledge of this burdened me before; now I glory in it because I have the more for you."

"Remember, I am older than yourself, and may early lose the beauty you love so well, leaving an old wife to burden your youth."

"What are a few years to me? Women like you grow lovelier with age, and you shall have a strong young husband to lean on all your life."

"Remember, I am not of your faith, and the priests will shut me out from your heaven."

"Let them prate as they will. Where you go I will go; Santa Paula shall be my madonna!"

"Remember, I am a deserted woman, and in the world we are going to my name may become the sport of that man's cruel tongue. Could you bear that patiently; and curb your fiery pride if I desired it?"

"Anything for you, Pauline!"

"One thing more. I give you my liberty; for a time give me forbearance in return, and though wed in haste woo me slowly, lest this sore heart of mine find even your light yoke heavy. Can you promise this, and wait till time has healed my wound, and taught me to be meek?"

"I swear to obey you in all things; make me what you will, for soul and body I am wholly yours henceforth."

"Faithful and true! I knew you would not fail me. Now go, Manuel. Tomorrow do your part resolutely as I shall do mine, and in a week we will begin the new life together. Ours is a strange betrothal, but it shall not lack some touch of tenderness from me. Love, good night."

Pauline bent till her bright hair mingled with the dark, kissed the boy on lips and forehead as a fond sister might have done, then put him gently from her; and like one in a blessed dream he went away to pace all night beneath her window, longing for the day.

As the echo of his steps died along the corridor, Pauline's eye fell on the paper lying where her lover flung it. At this sight all the softness vanished, the stern woman reappeared, and, crushing it in her hand with slow significance, she said low to herself, "This is an old, old story, but it shall have a new ending."

Chapter II

"What jewels will the senora wear tonight?"

"None, Dolores. Manuel has gone for flowers--he likes them best. You may go."

"But the senora's toilette is not finished; the sandals, the gloves, the garland yet remain."

"Leave them all; I shall not go down. I am tired of this endless folly. Give me that book and go."

The pretty Creole obeyed; and careless of Dolores' work, Pauline sank into the deep chair with a listless mien, turned the pages for a little, then lost herself in thoughts that seemed to bring no rest.

Silently the young husband entered and, pausing, regarded his wife with mingled pain and pleasure--pain to see her so spiritless, pleasure to see her so fair. She seemed unconscious of his presence till the fragrance of his floral burden betrayed him, and looking up to smile a welcome she met a glance that changed the sad dreamer into an excited actor, for it told her that the object of her search was found. Springing erect, she asked eagerly, "Manuel, is he here?"

"Yes."

"Alone?"

"His wife is with him."

"Is she beautiful?"

"Pretty, petite, and petulant."

"And he?"

"Unchanged: the same imposing figure and treacherous face, the same restless eye and satanic mouth. Pauline, let me insult him!"

"Not yet. Were they together?"

"Yes. He seemed anxious to leave her, but she called him back imperiously, and he came like one who dared not disobey."

"Did he see you?"

"The crowd was too dense, and I kept in the shadow."

"The wife's name? Did you learn it?"

"Barbara St. Just."

"Ah! I knew her once and will again. Manuel, am I beautiful tonight?"

"How can you be otherwise to me?"

"That is not enough. I must look my fairest to others, brilliant and blithe, a happy-hearted bride whose honeymoon is not yet over."

"For his sake, Pauline?"

"For yours. I want him to envy you your youth, your comeliness, your content; to see the man he once sneered at the husband of the woman he once loved; to recall impotent regret. I know his nature, and can stir him to his heart's core with a look, revenge myself with a word, and read the secrets of his life with a skill he cannot fathom."

"And when you have done all this, shall you be happier, Pauline?"

"Infinitely; our three weeks' search is ended, and the real interest of the plot begins. I have played the lover for your sake, now play the man of the world for mine. This is the moment we have waited for. Help me to make it successful. Come!

Crown me with your garland, give me the bracelets that were your wedding gift--none can be too brilliant for tonight. Now the gloves and fan. Stay, my sandals--you shall play Dolores and tie them on."

With an air of smiling coquetry he had never seen before, Pauline stretched out a truly Spanish foot and offered him its dainty covering. Won by the animation of her manner, Manuel forgot his misgivings and played his part with boyish spirit, hovering about his stately wife as no assiduous maid had ever done; for every flower was fastened with a word sweeter than itself, the white arms kissed as the ornaments went on, and when the silken knots were deftly accomplished, the lighthearted bridegroom performed a little dance of triumph about his idol, till she arrested him, beckoning as she spoke.

"Manuel, I am waiting to assume the last best ornament you have given me, my handsome husband." Then, as he came to her laughing with frank pleasure at her praise, she added, "You, too, must look your best and bravest now, and remember you must enact the man tonight. Before Gilbert wear your stateliest aspect, your tenderest to me, your courtliest to his wife. You possess dramatic skill. Use it for my sake, and come for your reward when this night's work is done."

The great hotel was swarming with life, ablaze with light, resonant with the tread of feet, the hum of voices, the musical din of the band, and full of the sights and sounds which fill such human hives at a fashionable watering place in the height of the season. As Manuel led his wife along the grand hall thronged with promenaders, his quick ear caught the whispered comments of the passers-by, and the fragmentary rumors concerning themselves amused him infinitely.

"***Mon ami!*** There are five bridal couples here tonight, and there is the handsomest, richest, and most enchanting of them all. The groom is not yet twenty, they tell me, and the bride still younger. Behold them!"

Manuel looked down at Pauline with a mirthful glance, but she had not heard.

"See, Belle! Cubans; own half the island between them. Splendid, aren't they? Look at the diamonds on her lovely arms, and his ravishing moustache. Isn't he your ideal of Prince Djalma, in The Wandering Jew?"

A pretty girl, forgetting propriety in interest, pointed as they passed. Manuel half-bowed to the audible compliment, and the blushing damsel vanished, but Pauline had not seen.

"Jack, there's the owner of the black span you fell into raptures over. My lord and lady look as highbred as their stud. We'll patronize them!"

Manuel muttered a disdainful "***Impertinente!***" between his teeth as he surveyed a brace of dandies with an air that augured ill for the patronage of Young America, but Pauline was unconscious of both criticism and reproof. A countercurrent held them stationary for a moment, and close behind them sounded a voice saying, confidentially, to some silent listener, "The Redmonds are here tonight, and I am curious to see how he bears his disappointment. You know he married for money, and was outwitted in the bargain; for his wife's fortune not only proves to be much less than he was led to believe, but is so tied up that he is entirely dependent upon her, and the bachelor debts he sold himself to liquidate still harass him, with a wife's reproaches to augment the affliction. To be ruled by a spoiled child's whims is a fit punishment for a man whom neither pride nor principle could curb before. Let us go and look at the unfortunate."

Pauline heard now. Manuel felt her start, saw her flush and pale, then her eye lit, and the dark expression he dreaded to see settled on her face as she whispered, like a satanic echo, "Let us also go and look at this unfortunate."

A jealous pang smote the young man's heart as he recalled the past.

"You pity him, Pauline, and pity is akin to love."

"I only pity what I respect. Rest content, my husband."

Steadily her eyes met his, and the hand whose only ornament was a wedding ring went to meet the one folded on his arm with a confiding gesture that made the action a caress.

"I will try to be, yet mine is a hard part," Manuel answered with a sigh, then silently they both paced on.

Gilbert Redmond lounged behind his wife's chair, looking intensely bored.

"Have you had enough of this folly, Babie?"

"No, we have but just come. Let us dance."

"Too late; they have begun."

"Then go about with me. It's very tiresome sitting here."

"It is too warm to walk in all that crowd, child."

"You are so indolent! Tell me who people are as they pass. I know no one here."

"Nor I."

But his act belied the words, for as they passed his lips he rose erect, with a smothered exclamation and startled face, as if a ghost had suddenly confronted him. The throng had thinned, and as his wife followed the direction of his glance, she saw no uncanny apparition to cause such evident dismay, but a woman fair-haired, violet-eyed, blooming and serene, sweeping down the long hall with noiseless grace. An air of sumptuous life pervaded her, the shimmer of bridal snow surrounded her, bridal gifts shone on neck and arms, and bridal happiness seemed to touch her with its tender charm as she looked up at her companion, as if there were but one human being in the world to her. This companion, a man slender and tall, with a face delicately dark as a fine bronze, looked back at her with eyes as eloquent as her own, while both spoke rapidly and low in the melodious language which seems made for lover's lips.

"Gilbert, who are they?"

There was no answer, and before she could repeat the question the approaching pair paused before her, and the beautiful woman offered her hand, saying, with inquiring smiles, "Barbara, have you forgotten your early friend, Pauline?"

Recognition came with the familiar name, and Mrs. Redmond welcomed the newcomer with a delight as unrestrained as if she were still the schoolgirl, Babie. Then, recovering herself, she said, with a pretty attempt at dignity, "Let me present my husband. Gilbert, come and welcome my friend Pauline Valary."

Scarlet with shame, dumb with conflicting emotions, and utterly deserted by self-possession, Redmond stood with downcast eyes and agitated mien, suffering a year's remorse condensed into a moment. A mute gesture was all the greeting he could offer. Pauline slightly bent her haughty head as she answered, in a voice frostily sweet, "Your wife mistakes. Pauline Valary died three weeks ago, and Pauline Laroche rose from her ashes. Manuel, my schoolmate, Mrs. Redmond; Gilbert you already know."

With the manly presence he could easily assume and which was henceforth to be his role in public, Manuel bowed courteously to the lady, coldly to the gentleman, and looked only at his wife. Mrs. Redmond, though childish, was observant; she glanced from face to face, divined a mystery, and spoke out at once.

"Then you have met before? Gilbert, you have never told me this."

"It was long ago--in Cuba. I believed they had forgotten me."

"I never forget." And Pauline's eye turned on him with a look he dared not meet.

Unsilenced by her husband's frown, Mrs. Redmond, intent on pleasing herself, drew her friend to the seat beside her as she said petulantly, "Gilbert tells me nothing, and I am constantly discovering things which might have given me pleasure had he only chosen to be frank. I've spoken of you often, yet he never betrayed the least knowledge of you, and I take it very ill of him, because I am sure he has not forgotten you. Sit here, Pauline, and let me tease you with questions, as I used to do so long ago. You were always patient with me, and though far more beautiful, your face is still the same kind one that comforted the little child at school. Gilbert, enjoy your friend, and leave us to ourselves until the dance is over."

Pauline obeyed; but as she chatted, skillfully leading the young wife's conversation to her own affairs, she listened to the two voices behind her, watched the two figures reflected in the mirror before her, and felt a secret pride in Manuel's address, for it was evident that the former positions were renewed.

The timid boy who had feared the sarcastic tongue of his guardian's guest, and shrunk from his presence to conceal the jealousy that was his jest, now stood beside his formal rival, serene and self-possessed, by far the manliest man of the two, for no shame daunted him, no fear oppressed him, no dishonorable deed left him at the mercy of another's tongue.

Gilbert Redmond felt this keenly, and cursed the falsehood which had placed him in such an unenviable position. It was vain to assume the old superiority that was forfeited; but too much a man of the world to be long discomforted by any contretemps like this, he rapidly regained his habitual ease of manner, and avoiding the perilous past clung to the safer present, hoping, by some unguarded look or word, to fathom the purpose of his adversary, for such he knew the husband of Pauline must be at heart. But Manuel schooled his features, curbed his tongue, and when his hot blood tempted him to point his smooth speech with a taunt, or offer a silent insult with the eye, he remembered Pauline, looked down on the graceful head below, and forgot all other passions in that of love.

"Gilbert, my shawl. The sea air chills me."

"I forgot it, Babie."

"Allow me to supply the want."

Mindful of his wife's commands, Manuel seized this opportunity to win a glance of commendation from her. And taking the downy mantle that hung upon his arm, he wrapped the frail girl in it with a care that made the act as cordial as courteous. Mrs. Redmond felt the charm of his manner with the quickness of a woman, and sent a reproachful glance at Gilbert as she said plaintively, "Ah! It is evident that my honeymoon is over, and the assiduous lover replaced by the negligent husband. Enjoy your midsummer night's dream while you may, Pauline, and be ready for the awakening that must come."

"Not to her, madame, for our honeymoon shall last till the golden wedding day comes round. Shall it not, carina?"

"There is no sign of waning yet, Manuel," and Pauline looked up into her husband's face with a genuine affection which made her own more beautiful and filled his with a visible content. Gilbert read the glance, and in that instant suffered the first pang of regret that Pauline had foretold. He spoke abruptly, longing to be away.

"Babie, we may dance now, if you will."

"I am going, but not with you--so give me my fan, and entertain Pauline till my return."

He unclosed his hand, but the delicately carved fan fell at his feet in a shower of ivory shreds--he had crushed it as he watched his first love with the bitter thought "It might have been!"

"Forgive me, Babie, it was too frail for use; you should choose a stronger."

"I will next time, and a gentler hand to hold it. Now, Monsieur Laroche, I am ready."

Mrs. Redmond rose in a small bustle of satisfaction, shook out her flounces, glanced at the mirror, then Manuel led her away; and the other pair were left alone. Both felt a secret agitation quicken their breath and thrill along their nerves, but the woman concealed it best. Gilbert's eye wandered restlessly to and fro, while Pauline fixed her own on his as quietly as if he were the statue in the niche behind him. For a moment he tried to seem unconscious of it, then essayed to meet and conquer it, but failed signally and, driven to his last resources by that steady gaze, resolved to speak out and have all over before his wife's return. Assuming the seat beside her, he said, impetuously, "Pauline, take off your mask as I do mine--we are alone now, and may see each other as we are."

Leaning deep into the crimson curve of the couch, with the indolent grace habitual to her, yet in strong contrast to the vigilant gleam of her eye, she swept her hand across her face as if obeying him, yet no change followed, as she said with a cold smile, "It is off; what next?"

"Let me understand you. Did my letter reach your hands?"

"A week before my marriage."

He drew a long breath of relief, yet a frown gathered as he asked, like one loath and eager to be satisfied, "Your love died a natural death, then, and its murder does not lie at my door?"

Pointing to the shattered toy upon the ground, she only echoed his own words. "It was too frail for use--I chose a stronger."

It wounded, as she meant it should; and the evil spirit to whose guidance she had yielded herself exulted to see his self-love bleed, and pride vainly struggle to conceal the stab. He caught the expression in her averted glance, bent suddenly a fixed and scrutinizing gaze upon her, asking, below his breath, "Then why are you here to tempt me with the face that tempted me a year ago?"

"I came to see the woman to whom you sold yourself. I have seen her, and am satisfied."

Such quiet contempt iced her tones, such pitiless satisfaction shone through the long lashes that swept slowly down, after her eye had met and caused his own to fall again, that Gilbert's cheek burned as if the words had been a blow, and mingled shame and anger trembled in his voice.

"Ah, you are quick to read our secret, for you possess the key. Have you no fear that I may read your own, and tell the world you sold your beauty for a name and fortune? Your bargain is a better one than mine, but I know you too well, though your fetters are diamonds and your master a fond boy."

She had been prepared for this, and knew she had a shield in the real regard she bore her husband, for though sisterly, it was sincere. She felt its value now, for it gave her courage to confront the spirit of retaliation she had roused, and calmness to answer the whispered taunt with an unruffled mien, as lifting her white arm she let its single decoration drop glittering to her lap.

"You see my 'fetters' are as loose as they are light, and nothing binds me but my will. Read my heart, if you can. You will find there contempt for a love so poor that it feared poverty; pity for a man who dared not face the world and conquer it, as a girl had done before him, and gratitude that I have found my 'master' in a truehearted boy, not a falsehearted man. If I am a slave, I never know it. Can you say as much?"

Her woman's tongue avenged her, and Gilbert owned his defeat. Pain quenched the ire of his glance, remorse subdued his pride, self- condemnation compelled him to ask, imploringly, "Pauline, when may I hope for pardon?"

"Never."

The stern utterance of the word dismayed him, and, like one shut out from hope, he rose, as if to leave her, but paused irresolutely, looked back, then sank down again, as if constrained against his will by a longing past control. If she had doubted her power this action set the doubt at rest, as the haughtiest nature she had known confessed it by a bittersweet complaint. Eyeing her wistfully, tenderly, Gilbert murmured, in the voice of long ago, "Why do I stay to wound and to be wounded by the hand that once caressed me? Why do I find more pleasure in your contempt than in another woman's praise, and feel myself transported into the delights of that irrecoverable past, now grown the sweetest, saddest memory of my life? Send me away, Pauline, before the old charm asserts its power, and I forget that I am not the happy lover of a year ago."

"Leave me then, Gilbert. Good night."

Half unconsciously, the former softness stole into her voice as it lingered on his name. The familiar gesture accompanied the words, the old charm did assert itself, and for an instant changed the cold woman into the ardent girl again. Gilbert did not go but, with a hasty glance down the deserted hall behind him, captured and kissed the hand he had lost, passionately whispering, "Pauline, I love you still, and that look assures me that you have forgiven, forgotten, and kept a place for me in that deep heart of yours. It is too late to deny it. I have seen the tender eyes again, and the sight has made me the proudest, happiest man that walks the world tonight, slave though I am."

Over cheek and forehead rushed the treacherous blood as the violet eyes filled and fell before his own, and in the glow of mingled pain and fear that stirred her blood, Pauline, for the first time, owned the peril of the task she had set herself, saw the dangerous power she possessed, and felt the buried passion faintly moving in its grave. Indignant at her own weakness, she took refuge in the memory of her wrong, controlled the rebel color, steeled the front she showed him, and with feminine skill mutely conveyed the rebuke she would not trust herself to utter, by stripping the glove from the hand he had touched and dropping it disdainfully as if unworthy of its place. Gilbert had not looked for such an answer, and while it baffled him it excited his man's spirit to rebel against her silent denial. With a bitter laugh he snatched up the glove.

"I read a defiance in your eye as you flung this down. I accept the challenge, and will keep gage until I prove myself the victor. I have asked for pardon. You refuse it. I have confessed my love. You scorn it. I have possessed myself of your secret, yet you deny it. Now we will try our strength together, and leave those children to their play."

"We are the children, and we play with edge tools. There has been enough of this, there must be no more." Pauline rose with her haughtiest mien, and the brief command, "Take me to Manuel."

Silently Gilbert offered his arm, and silently she rejected it.

"Will you accept nothing from me?"

"Nothing."

Side by side they passed through the returning throng till Mrs. Redmond joined them, looking blithe and bland with the exhilaration of gallantry and motion. Manuel's first glance was at Pauline, his second at her companion; there was a shadow upon the face of each, which seemed instantly to fall upon his own as he claimed his wife with a masterful satisfaction as novel as becoming, and which prompted her to whisper, "You enact your role to the life, and shall enjoy a foretaste of your reward at once. I want excitement; let us show these graceless, frozen people the true art of dancing, and electrify them with the life and fire of a Cuban valse."

Manuel kindled at once, and Pauline smiled stealthily as she glanced over her shoulder from the threshold of the dancing hall, for her slightest act, look, and word had their part to play in that night's drama.

"Gilbert, if you are tired I will go now."

"Thank you, I begin to find it interesting. Let us watch the dancers."

Mrs. Redmond accepted the tardy favor, wondering at his unwonted animation, for never had she seen such eagerness in his countenance, such energy in his manner as he pressed through the crowd and won a place where they could freely witness one of those exhibitions of fashionable figurante which are nightly to be seen at such resorts. Many couples were whirling around the white hall, but among them one pair circled with slowly increasing speed, in perfect time to the inspiring melody of trumpet, flute, and horn, that seemed to sound for them alone. Many paused to watch them, for they gave to the graceful pastime the enchantment which few have skill enough to lend it, and made it a spectacle of life-enjoying youth, to be remembered long after the music ceased and the agile feet were still.

Gilbert's arm was about his little wife to shield her from the pressure of the crowd, and as they stood his hold unconsciously tightened, till, marveling at this unwonted care, she looked up to thank him with a happy glance and discovered that his eye rested on a single pair, kindling as they approached, keenly scanning every gesture as they floated by, following them with untiring vigilance through the many-colored mazes they threaded with such winged steps, while his breath quickened, his hand kept time, and every sense seemed to own the intoxication of the scene. Sorrowfully she too watched this pair, saw their grace, admired their beauty, envied their happiness; for, short as her wedded life had been, the thorns already pierced her through the roses, and with each airy revolution of those figures, dark and bright, her discontent increased, her wonder deepened, her scrutiny grew keener, for she knew no common interest held her husband there, fascinated, flushed, and excited as if his heart beat responsive to the rhythmic rise and fall of that booted foot and satin slipper. The music ended with a crash, the crowd surged across the floor, and the spell was broken. Like one but half disenchanted, Gilbert stood a moment, then remembered his wife, and looking down met brown eyes, full of tears, fastened on his face.

"Tired so soon, Babie? Or in a pet because I cannot change myself into a thistle-down and float about with you, like Manuel and Pauline?"

"Neither; I was only wishing that you loved me as he loves her, and hoping he would never tire of her, they are so fond and charming now. How long have you known them--and where?"

"I shall have no peace until I tell you. I passed a single summer with them in a tropical paradise, where we swung half the day in hammocks, under tamarind and almond trees; danced half the night to music, of which this seems but a faint echo; and led a life of luxurious delight in an enchanted climate, where all is so beautiful and brilliant that its memory haunts a life as pressed flowers sweeten the leaves of a dull book."

"Why did you leave it then?"

"To marry you, child."

"That was a regretful sigh, as if I were not worth the sacrifice. Let us go back and enjoy it together."

"If you were dying for it, I would not take you to Cuba. It would be purgatory, not paradise, now."

"How stern you look, how strangely you speak. Would you not go to save your own life, Gilbert?"

"I would not cross the room to do that, much less the sea."

"Why do you both love and dread it? Don't frown, but tell me. I have a right to know."

"Because the bitterest blunder of my life was committed there--a blunder that I never can repair in this world, and may be damned for in the next. Rest satisfied with this, Babie, lest you prove like Bluebeard's wife, and make another skeleton in my closet, which has enough already."

Strange regret was in his voice, strange gloom fell upon his face; but though rendered doubly curious by the change, Mrs. Redmond dared not question further and, standing silent, furtively scanned the troubled countenance beside her. Gilbert spoke first, waking out of his sorrowful reverie with a start.

"Pauline is coming. Say adieu, not au revoir, for tomorrow we must leave this place."

His words were a command, his aspect one of stern resolve, though the intensest longing mingled with the dark look he cast on the approaching pair. The tone, the glance displeased his willful wife, who loved to use her power and exact obedience where she had failed to win affection, often ruling imperiously when a tender word would have made her happy to submit.

"Gilbert, you take no thought for my pleasures though you pursue your own at my expense. Your neglect forces me to find solace and satisfaction where I can, and you have forfeited your right to command or complain. I love Pauline, I am happy with her, therefore I shall stay until we tire of one another. I am a burden to you; go if you will."

"You know I cannot without you, Babie. I ask it as a favor. For my sake, for your own, I implore you to come away."

"Gilbert, do you love her?"

She seized his arm and forced an answer by the energy of her sharply whispered question. He saw that it was vain to dissemble, yet replied with averted head, "I did and still remember it."

"And she? Did she return your love?"

"I believed so; but she forgot me when I went. She married Manuel and is happy. Babie, let me go!"

"No! you shall stay and feel a little of the pain I feel when I look into your heart and find I have no place there. It is this which has stood between us and made all my efforts vain. I see it now and despise you for the falsehood you have shown me, vowing you loved no one but me until I married you, then letting me so soon discover that I was only an encumbrance to your enjoyment of the fortune I possessed. You treat me like a child, but I suffer like a woman, and you shall share my suffering, because you might have spared me, and you did not. Gilbert, you shall stay."

"Be it so, but remember I have warned you."

An exultant expression broke through the gloom of her husband's face as he answered with the grim satisfaction of one who gave restraint to the mind, and stood ready to follow whatever impulse should sway him next. His wife trembled inwardly at what she had done, but was too proud to recall her words and felt a certain bitter pleasure in the excitement of the new position she had taken, the new interest given to her listless life.

Pauline and Manuel found them standing silently together, for a moment had done the work of years and raised a barrier between them never to be swept away.

Mrs. Redmond spoke first, and with an air half resentful, half triumphant:

"Pauline, this morose husband of mine says we must leave tomorrow. But in some things I rule; this is one of them. Therefore we remain and go with you to the mountains when we are tired of the gay life here. So smile and submit, Gilbert, else these friends will count your society no favor. Would you not fancy, from the aspect he thinks proper to assume, that I had sentenced him to a punishment, not a pleasure?"

"Perhaps you have unwittingly, Babie. Marriage is said to cancel the follies of the past, but not those of the future, I believe; and, as there are many temptations to an idle man in a place like this, doubtless your husband is wise enough to own that he dares not stay but finds discretion the better part of valor."

Nothing could be softer than the tone in which these words were uttered, nothing sharper than the hidden taunt conveyed, but Gilbert only laughed a scornful laugh as he fixed his keen eyes full upon her and took her bouquet with the air of one assuming former rights.

"My dear Pauline, discretion is the last virtue I should expect to be accused of by you; but if valor consists in daring all things, I may lay claim to it without its 'better part,' for temptation is my delight--the stronger the better. Have no fears for me, my friend. I gladly accept Babie's decree and, ignoring the last ten years, intend to begin life anew, having discovered a sauce piquante which will give the stalest pleasures a redoubled zest. I am unfortunate tonight, and here is a second wreck; this I can rebuild happily. Allow me to do so, for I remember you once praised my skill in floral architecture."

With an air of eager gallantry in strange contrast to the malign expression of his countenance, Gilbert knelt to regather the flowers which a careless gesture of his own had scattered from their jeweled holder. His wife turned to speak to Manuel, and, yielding to the unconquerable anxiety his reckless manner awoke, Pauline whispered below her breath as she bent as if to watch the work, "Gilbert, follow your first impulse, and go tomorrow."

"Nothing shall induce me to."

"I warn you harm will come of it." "Let it come; I am past fear now."

"Shun me for Babie's sake, if not for your own."

"Too late for that; she is headstrong--let her suffer."

"Have you no power, Gilbert?"

"None over her, much over you."

"We will prove that!"

"We will!" Rapidly as words could shape them, these questions and answers fell, and with their utterance the last generous feeling died in Pauline's breast; for as she received the flowers, now changed from a love token to a battle gage, she saw the torn glove still crushed in Gilbert's hand, and silently accepted his challenge to the tournament so often held between man and woman--a tournament where the keen tongue is the lance, pride the shield, passion the fiery steed, and the hardest heart the winner of the prize, which seldom fails to prove a barren honor, ending in remorse.

Chapter III

For several days the Cubans were almost invisible, appearing only for a daily drive, a twilight saunter on the beach, or a brief visit to the ballroom, there to enjoy the excitement of the pastime in which they both excelled. Their apartments were in the quietest wing of the hotel, and from the moment of their occupancy seemed to acquire all the charms of home. The few guests admitted felt the atmosphere of poetry and peace that pervaded the nest which Love, the worker of miracles, had built himself even under that tumultuous roof. Strollers in the halls or along the breezy verandas often paused to listen to the music of instrument or voice which came floating out from these sequestered rooms. Frequent laughter and the murmur of conversation proved that ennui was unknown, and a touch of romance inevitably enhanced the interest wakened by the beautiful young pair, always together, always happy, never weary of the dolce far niente of this summer life.

In a balcony like a hanging garden, sheltered from the sun by blossoming shrubs and vines that curtained the green nook with odorous shade, Pauline lay indolently swinging in a gaily fringed hammock as she had been wont to do in Cuba, then finding only pleasure in the luxury of motion which now failed to quiet her unrest. Manuel had put down the book to which she no longer listened and, leaning his head upon his hand, sat watching her as she swayed to and fro with thoughtful eyes intent upon the sea, whose murmurous voice possessed a charm more powerful than his own. Suddenly he spoke:

"Pauline, I cannot understand you! For three weeks we hurried east and west to find this man, yet when found you shun him and seem content to make my life a heaven upon earth. I sometimes fancy that you have resolved to let the past sleep, but the hope dies as soon as born, for in moments like this I see that, though you devote yourself to me, the old purpose is unchanged, and I marvel why you pause."

Her eyes came back from their long gaze and settled on him full of an intelligence which deepened his perplexity. "You have not learned to know me yet; death is not more inexorable or time more tireless than I. This week has seemed one of indolent delight to you. To me it has been one of constant vigilance and labor, for scarcely a look, act, or word of mine has been without effect. At first I secluded myself that Gilbert might contrast our life with his and, believing us all and all to one another, find impotent regret his daily portion. Three days ago accident placed an unexpected weapon in my hand which I have used in silence, lest in spite of promises you should rebel and end his trial too soon. Have you no suspicion of my meaning?"

"None. You are more mysterious than ever, and I shall, in truth, believe you are the enchantress I have so often called you if your spells work invisibly."

"They do not, and I use no supernatural arts, as I will prove to you. Take my lorgnette that lies behind you, part the leaves where the green grapes hang thickest, look up at the little window in the shadowy angle of the low roof opposite, and tell me what you see."

"Nothing but a half-drawn curtain."

"Ah! I must try the ruse that first convinced me. Do not show yourself, but watch, and if you speak, let it be in Spanish."

Leaving her airy cradle, Pauline bent over the balcony as if to gather the climbing roses that waved their ruddy clusters in the wind. Before the third stem was broken Manuel whispered, "I see the curtain move; now comes the outline of a head, and now a hand, with some bright object in it. Santo Pablo! It is a man staring at you as coolly as if you were a lady in a balcony. What prying rascal is it?"

"Gilbert."

"Impossible! He is a gentleman."

"If gentlemen play the traitor and the spy, then he is one. I am not mistaken; for since the glitter of his glass first arrested me I have watched covertly, and several trials as successful as the present have confirmed the suspicion which Babie's innocent complaints of his long absences aroused. Now do you comprehend why I remained in these rooms with the curtains seldom drawn? Why I swung the hammock here and let you sing and read to me while I played with your hair or leaned upon your shoulder? Why I have been all devotion and made this balcony a little stage for the performance of our version of the honeymoon for one spectator?"

Still mindful of the eager eyes upon her, Pauline had been fastening the roses in her bosom as she spoke, and ended with a silvery laugh that made the silence musical with its heartsome sound. As she paused, Manuel flung down the lorgnette and was striding past her with ireful impetuosity, but the white arms took him captive, adding another figure to the picture framed by the green arch as she whispered decisively, "No farther! There must be no violence. You promised obedience and I exact it. Do you think detection to a man so lost to honor would wound as deeply as the sights which make his daily watch a torment? Or that a blow would be as hard to bear as the knowledge that his own act has placed you where you are and made him what he is? Silent contempt is the law now, so let this insult pass, unclench your hand and turn that defiant face to me, while I console you for submission with a kiss."

He yielded to the command enforced by the caress but drew her jealously from sight, and still glanced rebelliously through the leaves, asking with a frown, "Why show me this if I may not resent it? How long must I bear with this man? Tell me your design, else I shall mar it in some moment when hatred of him conquers love of you."

"I will, for it is tune, because though I have taken the first step you must take the second. I showed you this that you might find action pleasanter than rest, and you must bear with this man a little longer for my sake, but I will give you an amusement to beguile the time. Long ago you told me that Gilbert was a gambler. I would not believe it then, now I can believe anything, and you can convince the world of this vice of his as speedily as you will."

"Do you wish me to become a gambler that I may prove him one? I also told you that he was suspected of dishonorable play--shall I load the dice and mark the cards to catch him in his own snares?"

Manuel spoke bitterly, for his high spirit chafed at the task assigned him; womanly wiles seemed more degrading than the masculine method of retaliation, in which strength replaces subtlety and speedier vengeance brings speedier satisfaction. But Pauline, fast learning to play upon that mysterious instrument, the human heart, knew when to stimulate and when to soothe.

"Do not reproach me that I point out a safer mode of operation than your own. You would go to Gilbert and by a hot word, a rash act, put your life and my happiness into his hands, for though dueling is forbidden here, he would not hesitate to break all laws, human or divine, if by so doing he could separate us. What would you gain by it? If you kill him he is beyond our reach forever, and a crime remains to be atoned for. If he kill you your blood will be upon my head, and where should I find consolation for the loss of the one heart always true and tender?"

With the inexplicable prescience which sometimes foreshadows coming ills, she clung to him as if a vision of the future dimly swept before her, but he only saw the solicitude it was a sweet surprise to find he had awakened, and in present pleasure forgot past pain.

"You shall not suffer from this man any grief that I can shield you from, rest assured of that, my heart. I will be patient, though your ways are not mine, for the wrong was yours, and the retribution shall be such as you decree."

"Then hear your task and see the shape into which circumstances have molded my design. I would have you exercise a self-restraint that shall leave Gilbert no hold upon you, accept all invitations like that which you refused when we passed him on the threshold of the billiard room an hour ago, and seem to find in such amusements the same fascination as himself. Your skill in games of chance excels his, as you proved at home where these pastimes lose their disreputable aspect by being openly enjoyed. Therefore I would have you whet this appetite of his by losing freely at first--he will take a grim delight in lessening the fortune he covets--then exert all your skill till he is deeply in your debt. He has nothing but what is doled out to him by Babie's father, I find; he dare not ask help there for such a purpose; other resources have failed else he would not have married; and if the sum be large enough, it lays him under an obligation which will be a thorn in his flesh, the sharper for your knowledge of his impotence to draw it out. When this is done, or even while it is in progress, I would have you add the pain of a new jealousy to the old. He neglects this young wife of his, and she is eager to recover the affections she believes she once possessed. Help her, and teach Gilbert the value of what he now despises. You are young, comely, accomplished, and possessed of many graces more attractive than you are conscious of; your southern birth and breeding gift you with a winning warmth of manners in strong contrast to the colder natures around you; and your love for me lends an almost tender deference to your intercourse with all womankind. Amuse, console this poor girl, and show her husband what he should be; I have no fear of losing your heart nor need you fear for hers; she is one of those spaniel-like creatures who love the hand that strikes them and fawn upon the foot that spurns them."

"Am I to be the sole actor in the drama of deceit? While I woo Babie, what will you do, Pauline?"

"Let Gilbert woo me--have patience till you understand my meaning; he still loves me and believes I still return that love. I shall not undeceive him yet, but let silence seem to confess what I do not own in words. He fed me with false promises, let me build my life's happiness on baseless hopes, and rudely woke me when he could delude no longer, leaving me to find I had pursued a shadow. I will do the same. He shall follow me undaunted, undeterred by all obstacles, all ties; shall stake his last throw and lose it, for when the crowning moment comes I shall show him that through me he is made bankrupt in love, honor, liberty, and hope, tell him I am yours entirely and forever, then vanish like an ignis-fatuus, leaving him to the darkness of despair and defeat. Is not this a better retribution than the bullet that would give him peace at once?"

Boy, lover, husband though he was, Manuel saw and stood aghast at the baleful spirit which had enslaved this woman, crushing all generous impulses, withering all gentle charities, and making her the saddest spectacle this world can show--one human soul rebelling against Providence, to become the nemesis of another. Involuntarily he recoiled from her, exclaiming, "Pauline! Are you possessed of a devil?"

"Yes! One that will not be cast out till every sin, shame, and sorrow mental ingenuity can conceive and inflict has been heaped on that man's head. I thought I should be satisfied with one accusing look, one bitter word; I am not, for the evil genii once let loose cannot be recaptured. Once I ruled it, now it rules me, and there is no turning back. I have come under the law of fate, and henceforth the powers I possess will ban, not bless, for I am driven to whet and wield them as weapons which may win me success at the price of my salvation. It is not yet too late for you to shun the spiritual contagion I bear about me. Choose now, and abide by that choice without a shadow of turning, as I abide by mine. Take me as I am; help me willingly and unwillingly; and in the end receive the promised gift--years like the days you have called heaven upon earth. Or retract the vows you plighted, receive again the heart and name you gave me, and live unvexed by the stormy nature time alone can tame. Here is the ring. Shall I restore or keep it, Manuel?"

Never had she looked more beautiful as she stood there, an image of will, daring, defiant, and indomitable, with eyes darkened by intensity of emotion, voice half sad, half stern, and outstretched hand on which the wedding ring no longer shone. She felt her power, yet was wary enough to assure it by one bold appeal to the strongest element of her husband's character: passions, not principles, were the allies she desired, and before the answer came she knew that she had gained them at the cost of innocence and self-respect.

As Manuel listened, an expression like a dark reflection of her own settled on his face; a year of youth seemed to drop away; and with the air of one who puts fear behind him, he took the hand, replaced the ring, resolutely accepted the hard conditions, and gave all to love, only saying as he had said before, "Soul and body, I belong to you; do with me as you will."

A fortnight later Pauline sat alone, waiting for her husband. Under the pretext of visiting a friend, she had absented herself a week, that Manuel might give himself entirely to the distasteful task she set him. He submitted to the separation, wrote daily, but sent no tidings of his progress, told her nothing when they met that night, and had left her an hour before asking her to have patience till he could show his finished work. Now, with her eye upon the door, her ear alert to catch the coming step, her mind disturbed by contending hopes and fears, she sat waiting with the vigilant immobility of an Indian on the watch. She had not long to look and listen. Manuel entered hastily, locked the door, closed the windows, dropped the curtains, then paused in the middle of the room and broke into a low, triumphant laugh as he eyed his wife with an expression she had never seen in those dear eyes before. It startled her, and, scarcely knowing what to desire or dread, she asked eagerly, "You are come to tell me you have prospered."

"Beyond your hopes, for the powers of darkness seem to help us, and lead the man to his destruction faster than any wiles of ours can do. I am tired, let me lie here and rest. I have earned it, so when I have told all say, 'Love, you have done well,' and I am satisfied."

He threw himself along the couch where she still sat and laid his head in her silken lap, her cool hand on his hot forehead, and continued in a muffled voice.

"You know how eagerly Gilbert took advantage of my willingness to play, and soon how recklessly he pursued it, seeming to find the satisfaction you foretold, till, obeying your commands, I ceased losing and won sums which surprised me. Then you went, but I was not idle, and in the effort to extricate himself, Gilbert plunged deeper into debt; for my desire to please you seemed to gift me with redoubled skill. Two days ago I refused to continue the unequal conflict, telling him to give himself no uneasiness, for I could wait. You were right in thinking it would oppress him to be under any obligation to me, but wrong in believing he would endure, and will hardly be prepared for the desperate step he took to free himself. That night he played falsely, was detected, and though his opponent generously promised silence for Babie's sake, the affair stole out--he is shunned and this resource has failed. I thought he had no other, but yesterday he came to me with a strange expression of relief, discharged the debt to the last farthing, then hinted that my friendship with his wife was not approved by him and must cease. This proves that I have obeyed you in all things, though the comforting of Babie was an easy task, for, both loving you, our bond of sympathy and constant theme has been Pauline and her perfections."

"Hush! No praise--it is a mockery. I am what one man's perfidy has made; I may yet learn to be worthy of another man's devotion. What more, Manuel?"

"I thought I should have only a defeat to show you, but today has given me a strange success. At noon a gentleman arrived and asked for Gilbert. He was absent, but upon offering information relative to the time of his return, which proved my intimacy with him, this Seguin entered into conversation with me. His evident desire to avoid Mrs. Redmond and waylay her husband interested me, and when he questioned me somewhat closely concerning Gilbert's habits and movements of late, my suspicions were roused; and on mentioning the debt so promptly discharged, I received a confidence that startled me. In a moment of despair Gilbert had forged the name of his former friend, whom he believed abroad, had drawn the money and freed himself from my power, but not for long. The good fortune which has led him safely through many crooked ways seems to have deserted him in this strait. For the forgery was badly executed, inspection raised doubts, and Seguin, just returned, was at his banker's an hour after Gilbert, to prove the fraud; he came hither at once to accuse him of it and made me his confidant. What would you have had me do, Pauline? Time was short, and I could not wait for you."

"How can I tell at once? Why pause to ask? What did you do?"

"Took a leaf from your book and kept accusation, punishment, and power in my own hands, to be used in your behalf. I returned the money, secured the forged check, and prevailed on Seguin to leave the matter in my hands, while he departed as quietly as he had come. Babie's presence when we met tonight prevented my taking you into my counsels. I had prepared this surprise for you and felt a secret pride in working it out alone. An hour ago I went to watch for Gilbert. He came, I took him to his rooms, told him what I had done, added that compassion for his wife had actuated me. I left him saying the possession of the check was a full equivalent for the money, which I now declined to receive from such dishonorable hands. Are you satisfied, Pauline?"

With countenance and gestures full of exultation she sprang up to pace the room, exclaiming, as she seized the forged paper, "Yes, that stroke was superb! How strangely the plot thickens. Surely the powers of darkness are working with us and have put this weapon in our hands when that I forged proved useless. By means of this we have a hold upon him which nothing can destroy unless he escape by death. Will he, Manuel?"

"No; there was more wrath than shame in his demeanor when I accused him. He hates me too much to die yet, and had I been the only possessor of this fatal fact, I fancy it might have gone hard with me; for if ever there was murder in a man's heart it was in his when I showed him that paper and then replaced it next the little poniard you smile at me for wearing. This is over. What next, my queen?"

There was energy in the speaker's tone but none in attitude or aspect, as, still lying where she had left him, he pillowed his head upon his arm and turned toward her a face already worn and haggard with the feverish weariness that had usurped the blithe serenity which had been his chiefest charm a month ago. Pausing in her rapid walk, as if arrested by the change that seemed to strike her suddenly, she recalled her thoughts from the dominant idea of her life and, remembering the youth she was robbing of its innocent delights, answered the wistful look which betrayed the hunger of a heart she had never truly fed, as she knelt beside her husband and, laying her soft cheek to his, whispered in her tenderest accents, "I am not wholly selfish or ungrateful, Manuel. You shall rest now while I sing to you, and tomorrow we will go away among the hills and leave behind us for a time the dark temptation which harms you through me."

"No! Finish what you have begun. I will have all or nothing, for if we pause now you will bring me a divided mind, and I shall possess only the shadow of a wife. Take Gilbert and Babie with us, and end this devil's work without delay. Hark! What is that?"

Steps came flying down the long hall, a hand tried the lock, then beat impetuously upon the door, and a low voice whispered with shrill importunity, "Let me in! Oh, let me in!"

Manuel obeyed the urgent summons, and Mrs. Redmond, half dressed, with streaming hair and terror-stricken face, fled into Pauline's arms, crying incoherently, "Save me! Keep me! I never can go back to him; he said I was a burden and a curse, and wished I never had been born!"

"What has happened, Babie? We are your friends. Tell us, and let us comfort and protect you if we can."

But for a time speech was impossible, and the poor girl wept with a despairing vehemence sad to see, till their gentle efforts soothed her; and, sitting by Pauline, she told her trouble, looking oftenest at Manuel, who stood before them, as if sure of redress from him.

"When I left here an hour or more ago I found my rooms still empty, and, though I had not seen my husband since morning, I knew he would be displeased to find me waiting, so I cried myself to sleep and dreamed of the happy time when he was kind, till the sound of voices woke me. I heard Gilbert say, 'Babie is with your wife, her maid tells me; therefore we are alone here. What is this mysterious affair, Laroche?' That tempted me to listen, and then, Manuel, I learned all the shame and misery you so generously tried to spare me. How can I ever repay you, ever love and honor you enough for such care of one so helpless and forlorn as I?"

"I am repaid already. Let that pass, and tell what brings you here with such an air of fright and fear?"

"When you were gone he came straight to the inner room in search of something, saw me, and knew I must have heard all he had concealed from me so carefully. If you have ever seen him when that fierce temper of his grows ungovernable, you can guess what I endured. He said such cruel things I could not bear it, and cried out that I would come to you, for I was quite wild with terror, grief, and shame, that seemed like oil to fire. He swore I should not, and oh, Pauline, he struck me! See, if I do not tell the living truth!"

Trembling with excitement, Mrs. Redmond pushed back the wide sleeve of her wrapper and showed the red outline of a heavy hand. Manuel set his teeth and stamped his foot into the carpet with an indignant exclamation and the brief question, "Then you left him, Babie?"

"Yes, although he locked me in my room, saying the law gave him the right to teach obedience. I flung on these clothes, crept noiselessly along the balcony till the hall window let me in, and then I ran to you. He will come for me. Can he take me away? Must I go back to suffer any more?"

In the very act of uttering the words, Mrs. Redmond clung to Manuel with a cry of fear, for on the threshold stood her husband. A comprehensive glance seemed to stimulate his wrath and lend the hardihood wherewith to confront the three, saying sternly as he beckoned, "Babie, I am waiting for you."

She did not speak, but still clung to Manuel as if he were her only hope. A glance from Pauline checked the fiery words trembling on his lips, and he too stood silent while she answered with a calmness that amazed him:

"Your wife has chosen us her guardians, and I think you will scarcely venture to use force again with two such witnesses as these to prove that you have forfeited your right to her obedience and justify the step she has taken."

With one hand she uncovered the discolored arm, with the other held the forgery before him. For a moment Gilbert stood daunted by these mute accusations, but just then his ire burned hottest against Manuel; and believing that he could deal a double blow by wounding Pauline through her husband, he ignored her presence and, turning to the young man, asked significantly, "Am I to understand that you refuse me my wife, and prefer to abide by the consequences of such an act?"

Calmed by Pauline's calmness, Manuel only drew the trembling creature closer, and answered with his haughtiest mien, "I do; spare yourself the labor of insulting me, for having placed yourself beyond the reach of a gentleman's weapon, I shall accept no challenge from a--"

A soft hand at his lips checked the opprobrious word, as Babie, true woman through it all, whispered with a broken sob, "Spare him, for I loved him once."

Gilbert Redmond had a heart, and, sinful though it was, this generous forbearance wrung it with a momentary pang of genuine remorse, too swiftly followed by a selfish hope that all was not lost if through his wife he could retain a hold upon the pair which now possessed for him the strong attraction of both love and hate. In that brief pause this thought came, was accepted and obeyed, for, as if yielding to an uncontrollable impulse of penitent despair, he stretched his arms to his wife, saying humbly, imploringly, "Babie, come back to me, and teach me how I may retrieve the past. I freely confess I bitterly repent my manifold transgressions, and submit to your decree alone; but in executing justice, oh, remember mercy! Remember that I was too early left fatherless, motherless, and went astray for want of some kind heart to guide and cherish me. There is still time. Be compassionate and save me from myself. Am I not punished enough? Must death be my only comforter? Babie, when all others cast me off, will you too forsake me?"

"No, I will not! Only love me, and I can forgive, forget, and still be happy!"

Pauline was right. The spaniel-like nature still loved the hand that struck it, and Mrs. Redmond joyfully returned to the arms from which she had so lately fled. The tenderest welcome she had ever received from him welcomed the loving soul whose faith was not yet dead, for Gilbert felt the value this once neglected possession had suddenly acquired, and he held it close; yet as he soothed with gentle touch and tone, could not forbear a glance of triumph at the spectators of the scene.

Pauline met it with that inscrutable smile of hers, and a look of intelligence toward her husband, as she said, "Did I not prophesy truly, Manuel? Be kind to her, Gilbert, and when next we meet show us a happier wife than the one now sobbing on your shoulder. Babie, good night and farewell, for we are off to the mountains in the morning."

"Oh, let us go with you as you promised! You know our secret, you pity me and will help Gilbert to be what he should. I cannot live at home, and places like this will seem so desolate when you and Manuel are gone. May we, can we be with you a little longer?"

"If Gilbert wishes it and Manuel consents, we will bear and forbear much for your sake, my poor child."

Pauline's eye said, "Dare you go?" and Gilbert's answered, "Yes," as the two met with a somber fire in each; but his lips replied, "Anywhere with you, Babie," and Manuel took Mrs. Redmond's hand with a graceful warmth that touched her deeper than his words.

"Your example teaches me the beauty of compassion, and Pauline's friends are mine."

"Always so kind to me! Dear Manuel, I never can forget it, though I have nothing to return but this," and, like a grateful child, she lifted up her innocent face so wistfully he could only bend his tall head to receive the kiss she offered.

Gilbert's black brows lowered ominously at the sight, but he never spoke; and, when her good-nights were over, bowed silently and carried his little wife away, nestling to him as if all griefs and pains were banished by returning love.

"Poor little heart! She should have a smoother path to tread. Heaven grant she may hereafter; and this sudden penitence prove no sham." Manuel paused suddenly, for as if obeying an unconquerable impulse, Pauline laid a hand on either shoulder and searched his face with an expression which baffled his comprehension, though he bore it steadily till her eyes fell before his own, when he asked smilingly:

"Is the doubt destroyed, carina?"

"No; it is laid asleep."

Then as he drew her nearer, as if to make his peace for his unknown offense, she turned her cheek away and left him silently. Did she fear to find Babie's kiss upon his lips?

Chapter IV

The work of weeks is soon recorded, and when another month was gone these were the changes it had wrought. The four so strangely bound together by ties of suffering and sin went on their way, to the world's eye, blessed with every gracious gift, but below the tranquil surface rolled that undercurrent whose mysterious tides ebb and flow in human hearts unfettered by race or rank or time. Gilbert was a good actor, but, though he curbed his fitful temper, smoothed his mien, and sweetened his manner, his wife soon felt the vanity of hoping to recover that which never had been hers. Silently she accepted the fact and, uttering no complaint, turned to others for the fostering warmth without which she could not live. Conscious of a hunger like her own, Manuel could offer her sincerest sympathy, and soon learned to find a troubled pleasure in the knowledge that she loved him and her husband knew it, for his life of the emotions was rapidly maturing the boy into the man, as the fierce ardors of his native skies quicken the growth of wondrous plants that blossom in a night. Mrs. Redmond, as young in character as in years, felt the attraction of a nature generous and sweet, and yielded to it as involuntarily as an unsupported vine yields to the wind that blows it to the strong arms of a tree, still unconscious that a warmer sentiment than gratitude made his companionship the sunshine of her life. Pauline saw this, and sometimes owned within herself that she had evoked spirits which she could not rule, but her purpose drove her on, and in it she found a charm more perilously potent than before. Gilbert watched the three with a smile darker than a frown, yet no reproach warned his wife of the danger which she did not see; no jealous demonstration roused Manuel to rebel against the oppression of a presence so distasteful to him; no rash act or word gave Pauline power to banish him, though the one desire of his soul became the discovery of the key to the inscrutable expression of her eyes as they followed the young pair, whose growing friendship left their mates alone. Slowly her manner softened toward him, pity seemed to bridge across the gulf that lay between them, and in rare moments time appeared to have retraced its steps, leaving the tender woman of a year ago. Nourished by such unexpected hope, the early passion throve and strengthened until it became the mastering ambition of his life, and, only pausing to make assurance doubly sure, he waited the advent of the hour when he could "put his fortune to the touch and win or lose it all."

"Manuel, are you coming?"

He was lying on the sward at Mrs. Redmond's feet, and, waking from the reverie that held him, while his companion sang the love lay he was teaching her, he looked up to see his wife standing on the green slope before him. A black lace scarf lay over her blonde hair as Spanish women wear their veils, below it the violet eyes shone clear, the cheek glowed with the color fresh winds had blown upon their paleness, the lips parted with a wistful smile, and a knot of bright-hued leaves upon her bosom made a mingling of snow and fire in the dress, whose white folds swept the grass. Against a background of hoary cliffs and somber pines, this figure stood out like a picture of blooming womanhood, but Manuel saw three blemishes upon it--Gilbert had sketched her with that shadowy veil upon her head, Gilbert had swung himself across a precipice to reach the scarlet nosegay for her breast, Gilbert stood beside her with her hand upon his arm; and troubled by the fear that often haunted him since Pauline's manner to himself had grown so shy and sad, Manuel leaned and looked forgetful of reply, but Mrs. Redmond answered blithely:

"He is coming, but with me. You are too grave for us, so go your ways, talking wisely of heaven and earth, while we come after, enjoying both as we gather lichens, chase the goats, and meet you at the waterfall. Now senor, put away guitar and book, for I have learned my lesson; so help me with this unruly hair of mine and leave the Spanish for today."

They looked a pair of lovers as Manuel held back the long locks blowing in the wind, while Babie tied her hat, still chanting the burthen of the tender song she had caught so soon. A voiceless sigh stirred the ruddy leaves on Pauline's bosom as she turned away, but Gilbert embodied it in words, "They are happier without us. Let us go."

Neither spoke till they reached the appointed tryst. The others were not there, and, waiting for them, Pauline sat on a mossy stone, Gilbert leaned against the granite boulder beside her, and both silently surveyed a scene that made the heart glow, the eye kindle with delight as it swept down from that airy height, across valleys dappled with shadow and dark with untrodden forests, up ranges of majestic mountains, through gap after gap, each hazier than the last, far out into that sea of blue which rolls around all the world. Behind them roared the waterfall swollen with autumn rains and hurrying to pour itself into the rocky basin that lay boiling below, there to leave its legacy of shattered trees, then to dash itself into a deeper chasm, soon to be haunted by a tragic legend and go glittering away through forest, field, and intervale to join the river rolling slowly to the sea. Won by the beauty and the grandeur of the scene, Pauline forgot she was not alone, till turning, she suddenly became aware that while she scanned the face of nature her companion had been scanning hers. What he saw there she could not tell, but all restraint had vanished from his manner, all reticence from his speech, for with the old ardor in his eye, the old impetuosity in his voice, he said, leaning down as if to read her heart, "This is the moment I have waited for so long. For now you see what I see, that both have made a bitter blunder, and may yet repair it. Those children love each other; let them love, youth mates them, fortune makes them equals, fate brings them together that we may be free. Accept this freedom as I do, and come out into the world with me to lead the life you were born to enjoy."

With the first words he uttered Pauline felt that the time had come, and in the drawing of a breath was ready for it, with every sense alert, every power under full control, every feature obedient to the art which had become a second nature. Gilbert had seized her hand, and she did not draw it back; the sudden advent of the instant which must end her work sent an unwonted color to her cheek, and she did avert it; the exultation which flashed into her eyes made it unsafe to meet his own, and they drooped before him as if in shame or fear, her whole face woke and brightened with the excitement that stirred her blood. She did not seek to conceal it, but let him cheat himself with the belief that love touched it with such light and warmth, as she softly answered in a voice whose accents seemed to assure his hope.

"You ask me to relinquish much. What do you offer in return, Gilbert, that I may not for a second time find love's labor lost?"

It was a wily speech, though sweetly spoken, for it reminded him how much he had thrown away, how little now remained to give, but her mien inspired him, and nothing daunted, he replied more ardently than ever:

"I can offer you a heart always faithful in truth though not in seeming, for I never loved that child. I would give years of happy life to undo that act and be again the man you trusted. I can offer you a name which shall yet be an honorable one, despite the stain an hour's madness cast upon it. You once taunted me with cowardice because I dared not face the world and conquer it. I dare do that now; I long to escape from this disgraceful servitude, to throw myself into the press, to struggle and achieve for your dear sake. I can offer you strength, energy, devotion-- three gifts worthy any woman's acceptance who possesses power to direct, reward, and enjoy them as you do, Pauline. Because with your presence for my inspiration, I feel that I can retrieve my faultful past, and with time become God's noblest work--an honest man. Babie never could exert this influence over me. You can, you will, for now my earthly hope is in your hands, my soul's salvation in your love."

If that love had not died a sudden death, it would have risen up to answer him as the one sincere desire of an erring life cried out to her for help, and this man, as proud as sinful, knelt down before her with a passionate humility never paid at any other shrine, human or divine. It seemed to melt and win her, for he saw the color ebb and flow, heard the rapid beating of her heart, felt the hand tremble in his own, and received no denial but a lingering doubt, whose removal was a keen satisfaction to himself.

"Tell me, before I answer, are you sure that Manuel loves Babie?"

"I am; for every day convinces me that he has outlived the brief delusion, and longs for liberty, but dares not ask it. Ah! that pricks pride! But it is so. I have watched with jealous vigilance and let no sign escape me; because in his infidelity to you lay my chief hope. Has he not grown melancholy, cold, and silent? Does he not seek Babie and, of late, shun you? Will he not always yield his place to me without a token of displeasure or regret? Has he ever uttered reproach, warning, or command to you, although he knows I was and am your lover? Can you deny these proofs, or pause to ask if he will refuse to break the tie that binds him to a woman, whose superiority in all things keeps him a subject where he would be a king? You do not know the heart of man if you believe he will not bless you for his freedom."

Like the cloud which just then swept across the valley, blotting out its sunshine with a gloomy shadow, a troubled look flitted over Pauline's face. But if the words woke any sleeping fear she cherished, it was peremptorily banished, for scarcely had the watcher seen it than it was gone. Her eyes still shone upon the ground, and still she prolonged the bittersweet delight at seeing this humiliation of both soul and body by asking the one question whose reply would complete her sad success.

"Gilbert, do you believe I love you still?"

"I know it! Can I not read the signs that proved it to me once? Can I forget that, though you followed me to pity and despise, you have remained to pardon and befriend? Am I not sure that no other power could work the change you have wrought in me? I was learning to be content with slavery, and slowly sinking into that indolence of will which makes submission easy. I was learning to forget you, and be resigned to hold the shadow when the substance was gone, but you came, and with a look undid my work, with a word destroyed my hard-won peace, with a touch roused the passion which was not dead but sleeping, and have made this month of growing certainty to be the sweetest in my life--for I believed all lost, and you showed me that all was won. Surely that smile is propitious! and I may hope to hear the happy confirmation of my faith from lips that were formed to say 'I love!'"

She looked up then, and her eyes burned on him, with an expression which made his heart leap with expectant joy, as over cheek and forehead spread a glow of womanly emotion too genuine to be feigned, and her voice thrilled with the fervor of that sentiment which blesses life and outlives death.

"Yes, I love; not as of old, with a girl's blind infatuation, but with the warmth and wisdom of heart, mind, and soul--love made up of honor, penitence and trust, nourished in secret by the better self which lingers in the most tried and tempted of us, and now ready to blossom and bear fruit, if God so wills. I have been once deceived, but faith still endures, and I believe that I may yet earn this crowning gift of a woman's life for the man who shall make my happiness as I make his--who shall find me the prouder for past coldness, the humbler for past pride --whose life shall pass serenely loving. And that beloved is--my husband." If she had lifted her white hand and stabbed him, with that smile upon her face, it would not have shocked him with a more pale dismay than did those two words as Pauline shook him off and rose up, beautiful and stern as an avenging angel. Dumb with an amazement too fathomless for words, he knelt there motionless and aghast. She did not speak. And, passing his hand across his eyes as if he felt himself the prey to some delusion, he rose slowly, asking, half incredulously, half imploringly, "Pauline, this is a jest?"

"To me it is; to you--a bitter earnest."

A dim foreboding of the truth fell on him then, and with it a strange sense of fear; for in this apparition of human judgment he seemed to receive a premonition of the divine. With a sudden gesture of something like entreaty, he cried out, as if his fate lay in her hands, "How will it end? how will it end?"

"As it began--in sorrow, shame and loss." Then, in words that fell hot and heavy on the sore heart made desolate, she poured out the dark history of the wrong and the atonement wrung from him with such pitiless patience and inexorable will. No hard fact remained unrecorded, no subtle act unveiled, no hint of her bright future unspared to deepen the gloom of his. And when the final word of doom died upon the lips that should have awarded pardon, not punishment, Pauline tore away the last gift he had given, and dropping it to the rocky path, set her foot upon it, as if it were the scarlet badge of her subjection to the evil spirit which had haunted her so long, now cast out and crushed forever.

Gilbert had listened with a slowly gathering despair, which deepened to the blind recklessness that comes to those whose passions are their masters, when some blow smites but cannot subdue. Pale to his very lips, with the still white wrath, so much more terrible to witness than the fiercest ebullition of the ire that flames and feeds like a sudden fire, he waited till she ended, then used the one retaliation she had left him. His hand went to his breast, a tattered glove flashed white against the cliff as he held it up before her, saying, in a voice that rose gradually till the last words sounded clear above the waterfall's wild song:

"It was well and womanly done, Pauline, and I could wish Manuel a happy life with such a tender, frank, and noble wife; but the future which you paint so well never shall be his. For, by the Lord that hears me! I swear I will end this jest of yours in a more bitter earnest than you prophesied. Look; I have worn this since the night you began the conflict, which has ended in defeat to me, as it shall to you. I do not war with women, but you shall have one man's blood upon your soul, for I will goad that tame boy to rebellion by flinging this in his face and taunting him with a perfidy blacker than my own. Will that rouse him to forget your commands and answer like a man?"

"Yes!"

The word rang through the air sharp and short as a pistol shot, a slender brown hand wrenched the glove away, and Manuel came between them. Wild with fear, Mrs. Redmond clung to him. Pauline sprang before him, and for a moment the two faced each other, with a year's smoldering jealousy and hate blazing in fiery eyes, trembling in clenched hands, and surging through set teeth in defiant speech.

"This is the gentleman who gambles his friend to desperation, and skulks behind a woman, like the coward he is," sneered Gilbert.

"Traitor and swindler, you lie!" shouted Manuel, and, flinging his wife behind him, he sent the glove, with a stinging blow, full in his opponent's face.

Then the wild beast that lurks in every strong man's blood leaped up in Gilbert Redmond's, as, with a single gesture of his sinewy right arm he swept Manuel to the verge of the narrow ledge, saw him hang poised there one awful instant, struggling to save the living weight that weighed him down, heard a heavy plunge into the black pool below, and felt that thrill of horrible delight which comes to murderers alone.

So swift and sure had been the act it left no time for help. A rush, a plunge, a pause, and then two figures stood where four had been--a man and woman staring dumbly at each other, appalled at the dread silence that made high noon more ghostly than the deepest night. And with that moment of impotent horror, remorse, and woe, Pauline's long punishment began.

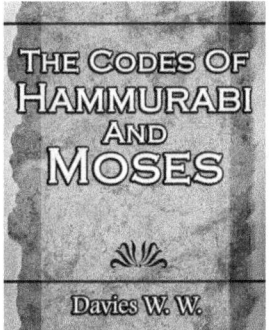

The Codes Of Hammurabi And Moses
W. W. Davies

QTY

The discovery of the Hammurabi Code is one of the greatest achievements of archaeology, and is of paramount interest, not only to the student of the Bible, but also to all those interested in ancient history...

Religion   **ISBN:** *1-59462-338-4*   **Pages:132**

MSRP $12.95

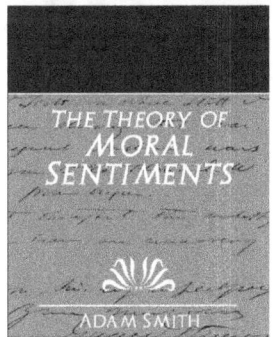

The Theory of Moral Sentiments
Adam Smith

QTY

This work from 1749. contains original theories of conscience amd moral judgment and it is the foundation for systemof morals.

Philosophy ISBN: *1-59462-777-0*   **Pages:536**

MSRP $19.95

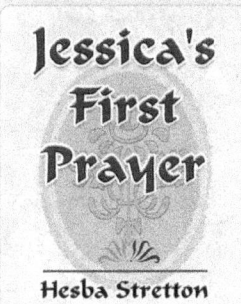

Jessica's First Prayer
Hesba Stretton

QTY

In a screened and secluded corner of one of the many railway-bridges which span the streets of London there could be seen a few years ago, from five o'clock every morning until half past eight, a tidily set-out coffee-stall, consisting of a trestle and board, upon which stood two large tin cans, with a small fire of charcoal burning under each so as to keep the coffee boiling during the early hours of the morning when the work-people were thronging into the city on their way to their daily toil...

Pages:84

Childrens   ISBN: *1-59462-373-2*   *MSRP $9.95*

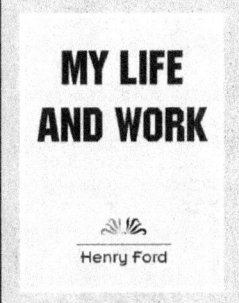

My Life and Work
Henry Ford

QTY

Henry Ford revolutionized the world with his implementation of mass production for the Model T automobile. Gain valuable business insight into his life and work with his own auto-biography... "We have only started on our development of our country we have not as yet, with all our talk of wonderful progress, done more than scratch the surface. The progress has been wonderful enough but..."

Pages:300

Biographies/   **ISBN:** *1-59462-198-5*   *MSRP $21.95* www.bookjungle.com *email: sales@bookjungle.com fax: 630-214-0564 mail: Book Jungle PO Box 2226 Champaign, IL 61825*

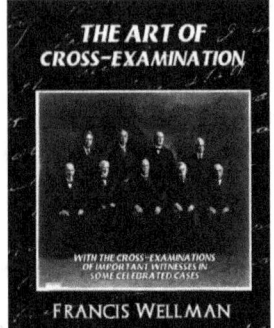

The Art of Cross-Examination
Francis Wellman

QTY

I presume it is the experience of every author, after his first book is published upon an important subject, to be almost overwhelmed with a wealth of ideas and illustrations which could readily have been included in his book, and which to his own mind, at least, seem to make a second edition inevitable. Such certainly was the case with me; and when the first edition had reached its sixth impression in five months, I rejoiced to learn that it seemed to my publishers that the book had met with a sufficiently favorable reception to justify a second and considerably enlarged edition. ..

Reference   ISBN: *1-59462-647-2*

Pages:412

MSRP $19.95

On the Duty of Civil Disobedience
Henry David Thoreau

QTY

Thoreau wrote his famous essay, On the Duty of Civil Disobedience, as a protest against an unjust but popular war and the immoral but popular institution of slave-owning. He did more than write—he declined to pay his taxes, and was hauled off to gaol in consequence. Who can say how much this refusal of his hastened the end of the war and of slavery ?

Law   ISBN: *1-59462-747-9*

Pages:48

MSRP $7.45

Dream Psychology Psychoanalysis for Beginners
Sigmund Freud

QTY

Sigmund Freud, born Sigismund Schlomo Freud (May 6, 1856 - September 23, 1939), was a Jewish-Austrian neurologist and psychiatrist who co-founded the psychoanalytic school of psychology. Freud is best known for his theories of the unconscious mind, especially involving the mechanism of repression; his redefinition of sexual desire as mobile and directed towards a wide variety of objects; and his therapeutic techniques, especially his understanding of transference in the therapeutic relationship and the presumed value of dreams as sources of insight into unconscious desires.

Psychology   ISBN: *1-59462-905-6*

Pages:196

MSRP $15.45

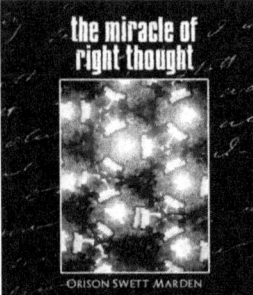

The Miracle of Right Thought
Orison Swett Marden

QTY

Believe with all of your heart that you will do what you were made to do. When the mind has once formed the habit of holding cheerful, happy, prosperous pictures, it will not be easy to form the opposite habit. It does not matter how improbable or how far away this realization may see, or how dark the prospects may be, if we visualize them as best we can, as vividly as possible, hold tenaciously to them and vigorously struggle to attain them, they will gradually become actualized, realized in the life. But a desire, a longing without endeavor, a yearning abandoned or held indifferently will vanish without realization.

Self Help   ISBN: *1-59462-644-8*

Pages:360

MSRP $25.45

The Rosicrucian Cosmo-Conception Mystic Christianity by *Max Heindel* ISBN: *1-59462-188-8* **$38.95**
The Rosicrucian Cosmo-conception is not dogmatic, neither does it appeal to any other authority than the reason of the student. It is: not controversial, but is: sent forth in the, hope that it may help to clear... New Age/Religion Pages 646

Abandonment To Divine Providence by *Jean-Pierre de Caussade* ISBN: *1-59462-228-0* **$25.95**
"The Rev. Jean Pierre de Caussade was one of the most remarkable spiritual writers of the Society of Jesus in France in the 18th Century. His death took place at Toulouse in 1751. His works have gone through many editions and have been republished... Inspirational/Religion Pages 400

Mental Chemistry by *Charles Haanel* ISBN: *1-59462-192-6* **$23.95**
Mental Chemistry allows the change of material conditions by combining and appropriately utilizing the power of the mind. Much like applied chemistry creates something new and unique out of careful combinations of chemicals the mastery of mental chemistry... New Age Pages 354

The Letters of Robert Browning and Elizabeth Barret Barrett 1845-1846 vol II ISBN: *1-59462-193-4* **$35.95**
by *Robert Browning and Elizabeth Barrett* Biographies Pages 596

Gleanings In Genesis (volume I) by *Arthur W. Pink* ISBN: *1-59462-130-6* **$27.45**
Appropriately has Genesis been termed "the seed plot of the Bible" for in it we have, in germ form, almost all of the great doctrines which are afterwards fully developed in the books of Scripture which follow... Religion/Inspirational Pages 420

The Master Key by *L. W. de Laurence* ISBN: *1-59462-001-6* **$30.95**
In no branch of human knowledge has there been a more lively increase of the spirit of research during the past few years than in the study of Psychology, Concentration and Mental Discipline. The requests for authentic lessons in Thought Control, Mental Discipline and... New Age/Business Pages 422

The Lesser Key Of Solomon Goetia by *L. W. de Laurence* ISBN: *1-59462-092-X* **$9.95**
This translation of the first book of the "Lernegton" which is now for the first time made accessible to students of Talismanic Magic was done, after careful collation and edition, from numerous Ancient Manuscripts in Hebrew, Latin, and French... New Age/Occult Pages 92

Rubaiyat Of Omar Khayyam by *Edward Fitzgerald* ISBN:*1-59462-332-5* **$13.95**
Edward Fitzgerald, whom the world has already learned, in spite of his own efforts to remain within the shadow of anonymity, to look upon as one of the rarest poets of the century, was born at Bredfield, in Suffolk, on the 31st of March, 1809. He was the third son of John Purcell... Music Pages 172

Ancient Law by *Henry Maine* ISBN: *1-59462-128-4* **$29.95**
The chief object of the following pages is to indicate some of the earliest ideas of mankind, as they are reflected in Ancient Law, and to point out the relation of those ideas to modern thought. Religion/History Pages 452

Far-Away Stories by *William J. Locke* ISBN: *1-59462-129-2* **$19.45**
"Good wine needs no bush, but a collection of mixed vintages does. And this book is just such a collection. Some of the stories I do not want to remain buried for ever in the museum files of dead magazine-numbers an author's not unpardonable vanity..." Fiction Pages 272

Life of David Crockett by *David Crockett* ISBN: *1-59462-250-7* **$27.45**
"Colonel David Crockett was one of the most remarkable men of the times in which he lived. Born in humble life, but gifted with a strong will, an indomitable courage, and unremitting perseverance... Biographies/New Age Pages 424

Lip-Reading by *Edward Nitchie* ISBN: *1-59462-206-X* **$25.95**
Edward B. Nitchie, founder of the New York School for the Hard of Hearing, now the Nitchie School of Lip-Reading, Inc, wrote "LIP-READING Principles and Practice". The development and perfecting of this meritorious work on lip-reading was an undertaking... How-to Pages 400

A Handbook of Suggestive Therapeutics, Applied Hypnotism, Psychic Science ISBN: *1-59462-214-0* **$24.95**
by *Henry Munro* Health/New Age/Health/Self-help Pages 376

A Doll's House: and Two Other Plays by *Henrik Ibsen* ISBN: *1-59462-112-8* **$19.95**
Henrik Ibsen created this classic when in revolutionary 1848 Rome. Introducing some striking concepts in playwriting for the realist genre, this play has been studied the world over. Fiction/Classics/Plays 308

The Light of Asia by *sir Edwin Arnold* ISBN: *1-59462-204-3* **$13.95**
In this poetic masterpiece, Edwin Arnold describes the life and teachings of Buddha. The man who was to become known as Buddha to the world was born as Prince Gautama of India but he rejected the worldly riches and abandoned the reigns of power when... Religion/History/Biographies Pages 170

The Complete Works of Guy de Maupassant by *Guy de Maupassant* ISBN: *1-59462-157-8* **$16.95**
"For days and days, nights and nights, I had dreamed of that first kiss which was to consecrate our engagement, and I knew not on what spot I should put my lips..." Fiction/Classics Pages 240

The Art of Cross-Examination by *Francis L. Wellman* ISBN: *1-59462-309-0* **$26.95**
Written by a renowned trial lawyer, Wellman imparts his experience and uses case studies to explain how to use psychology to extract desired information through questioning. How-to/Science/Reference Pages 408

Answered or Unanswered? by *Louisa Vaughan* ISBN: *1-59462-248-5* **$10.95**
Miracles of Faith in China Religion Pages 112

The Edinburgh Lectures on Mental Science (1909) by *Thomas* ISBN: *1-59462-008-3* **$11.95**
This book contains the substance of a course of lectures recently given by the writer in the Queen Street Hall, Edinburgh. Its purpose is to indicate the Natural Principles governing the relation between Mental Action and Material Conditions... New Age/Psychology Pages 148

Ayesha by *H. Rider Haggard* ISBN: *1-59462-301-5* **$24.95**
Verily and indeed it is the unexpected that happens! Probably if there was one person upon the earth from whom the Editor of this, and of a certain previous history, did not expect to hear again... Classics Pages 380

Ayala's Angel by *Anthony Trollope* ISBN: *1-59462-352-X* **$29.95**
The two girls were both pretty, but Lucy who was twenty-one who supposed to be simple and comparatively unattractive, whereas Ayala was credited, as her Bombwhat romantic name might show, with poetic charm and a taste for romance. Ayala when her father died was nineteen... Fiction Pages 484

The American Commonwealth by *James Bryce* ISBN: *1-59462-286-8* **$34.45**
An interpretation of American democratic political theory. It examines political mechanics and society from the perspective of Scotsman James Bryce Politics Pages 572

Stories of the Pilgrims by *Margaret P. Pumphrey* ISBN: *1-59462-116-0* **$17.95**
This book explores pilgrims religious oppression in England as well as their escape to Holland and eventual crossing to America on the Mayflower, and their early days in New England... History Pages 268

QTY

The Fasting Cure *by Sinclair Upton*　　　　　　　ISBN: *1-59462-222-1*　**$13.95**
In the Cosmopolitan Magazine for May, 1910, and in the Contemporary Review (London) for April, 1910, I published an article dealing with my experiences in fasting. I have written a great many magazine articles, but never one which attracted so much attention... New Age/Self Help/Health Pages 164

Hebrew Astrology *by Sepharial*　　　　　　　ISBN: *1-59462-308-2*　**$13.45**
In these days of advanced thinking it is a matter of common observation that we have left many of the old landmarks behind and that we are now pressing forward to greater heights and to a wider horizon than that which represented the mind-content of our progenitors...　Astrology Pages 144

Thought Vibration or The Law of Attraction in the Thought World　　ISBN: *1-59462-127-6*　**$12.95**
by William Walker Atkinson　　　　　　　*Psychology/Religion Pages 144*

Optimism *by Helen Keller*　　　　　　　ISBN: *1-59462-108-X*　**$15.95**
Helen Keller was blind, deaf, and mute since 19 months old, yet famously learned how to overcome these handicaps, communicate with the world, and spread her lectures promoting optimism. An inspiring read for everyone...　Biographies/Inspirational Pages 84

Sara Crewe *by Frances Burnett*　　　　　　　ISBN: *1-59462-360-0*　**$9.45**
In the first place, Miss Minchin lived in London. Her home was a large, dull, tall one, in a large, dull square, where all the houses were alike, and all the sparrows were alike, and where all the door-knockers made the same heavy sound...　Childrens/Classic Pages 88

The Autobiography of Benjamin Franklin *by Benjamin Franklin*　　ISBN: *1-59462-135-7*　**$24.95**
The Autobiography of Benjamin Franklin has probably been more extensively read than any other American historical work, and no other book of its kind has had such ups and downs of fortune. Franklin lived for many years in England, where he was agent...　Biographies/History Pages 332

Name	
Email	
Telephone	
Address	
City, State ZIP	

☐ Credit Card　　　　☐ Check / Money Order

Credit Card Number	
Expiration Date	
Signature	

Please Mail to:　Book Jungle
PO Box 2226
Champaign, IL 61825
or Fax to:　　630-214-0564

ORDERING INFORMATION
web: *www.bookjungle.com*
email: *sales@bookjungle.com*
fax: *630-214-0564*
mail: *Book Jungle PO Box 2226 Champaign, IL 61825*
or PayPal *to sales@bookjungle.com*

Please contact us for bulk discounts

DIRECT-ORDER TERMS
**20% Discount if You Order
Two or More Books**
Free Domestic Shipping!
Accepted: Master Card, Visa,
Discover, American Express

www.ingramcontent.com/pod-product-compliance
Lightning Source LLC
Chambersburg PA
CBHW081148170626
46809CB00010B/3142

9 781438 517285